garage

post
office

health
centre

church

primary school

nursery school

police station

This Topsy and Tim book belongs to

_____

Hello, I'm Topsy!

Hello, I'm Tim!

Topsy and Tim

My First Story Collection

Illustrations by Belinda Worsley

A catalogue record for this book is available from the British Library

Published by Ladybird Books Ltd
A Penguin Company
Penguin Books Ltd., 80 Strand, London WC2R 0RL, UK
Penguin Books Australia Ltd., 707 Collins Street, Melbourne, Victoria 3008, Australia
Penguin Group (NZ) 67 Apollo Drive, Rosedale, North Shore 0632, New Zealand

001

Topsy and Tim Learn to Swim © Jean and Gareth Adamson MCMXCV
Topsy and Tim Go on an Aeroplane © Jean and Gareth Adamson MCMXCV
Topsy and Tim Start School © Jean and Gareth Adamson MCMXCV
Topsy and Tim Go to the Doctor © Jean and Gareth Adamson MCMXCV
Topsy and Tim Go Camping © Jean and Gareth Adamson MMVII
This collection © Jean and Gareth Adamson MMXIV
The moral rights of the author/illustrator have been asserted

ISBN: 978-0-72329-777-2
Printed in China

www.topsyandtim.com

Topsy and Tim

My First Story Collection

By Jean and Gareth Adamson

Contents

Topsy and Tim
Learn to Swim

Topsy and Tim were learning to swim. Mummy took them to the swimming pool nearly every day.

Mummy helped them put on their swimming things and blow up their armbands. She put their clothes safely in a locker.

On the way to the pool there were showers,
to make sure they were nice and clean.

There was a small pool for beginners like Topsy
and Tim. It was full of happy, noisy children.
"Race you to the water!" shouted Topsy.
Topsy's feet skidded. Mr Pollack the swimming
instructor rushed to save her.

"Never run near the pool," he said. "The floor is wet and slippery and it's very hard if you fall and bang your head."

Topsy and Tim went down the steps into the pool.
Mummy went in with them. The water came up to
Topsy and Tim's middles.

They held on to the rail and kicked as hard as they could. Mummy did get splashed. "Stretch your legs out," she said.

"Now let me see you swim dog-paddle," said Mummy. Topsy paddled like a puppy. Her armbands helped her to float.

Tim paddled hard. He splashed more than Topsy, but his legs kept sinking.

"Do you think you could swim without your armbands?" asked Mummy.
"Of course," shouted Tim.
"I'm a champion swimmer."

First Topsy stood in the water a few steps from
the side. Then she pushed forward in the water
and dog-paddled to the hand rail.
"Well done, Topsy," said Mummy.
"You can really swim now."

Then it was Tim's turn. He tried hard... but his feet would not float.
"Never mind," said Mummy. "You must put your armbands back on."

"Can I help?" said a kind voice. It was Mr Pollack, the swimming instructor. He told Tim to bob right down until the water was up to his chin.
"Now walk along and pull the water back with your hands," he said.

Tim paddled hard with his hands, then he
kicked up and down with his legs.
"Look at me," he gasped. "I'm swimming!"
And he really was.

Mummy helped them to get dressed and dry their hair. "Won't Dad be surprised when we tell him we can swim without our armbands," said Tim.

Dad was waiting for them in the
snack bar.
"Dad, we can swim!" cried Topsy.
Dad was pleased.

26

He pointed to a poster on the wall.
"There's going to be a swimming competition,"
he said. "You can swim in the beginners' race,
Topsy and Tim."

The next week Dad and Mummy and Topsy
and Tim went to the big pool for the swimming
competition.
There were short races.
There were long races.

There was a race for children swimming on their backs.
Last of all there was the beginners' race in the beginners' pool.

Mr Pollack blew his whistle to start the race.
Topsy swam dog-paddle as fast as she could.
Tim was left behind – but he knew what to do.

He bobbed right down in the water until it reached his chin, then he paddled hard with his hands and feet. Everyone cheered as the children swam slowly across the pool.

Topsy and Tim didn't win the race, but everyone got a Beginners' Badge because they had all reached the other side.

Now turn the page and help
Topsy and Tim solve a puzzle.

Can you help Topsy and Tim swim to Mummy at the other side of the pool? They must try not to bump into the other people.

35

Topsy and Tim
Go on an Aeroplane

Topsy and Tim were off on their summer holidays.
They were going in an aeroplane.

The airport was very big.
Topsy and Tim had a long ride in a
bus to reach the terminal building.

Then they had a long ride on an escalator to get to the right part of the building.

Their luggage went for a long ride
too, on a moving platform.

Topsy and Tim watched an aeroplane land.
It looked much bigger when it was not in the sky.
The door was high off the ground.
"How will the people get out?" asked Topsy.

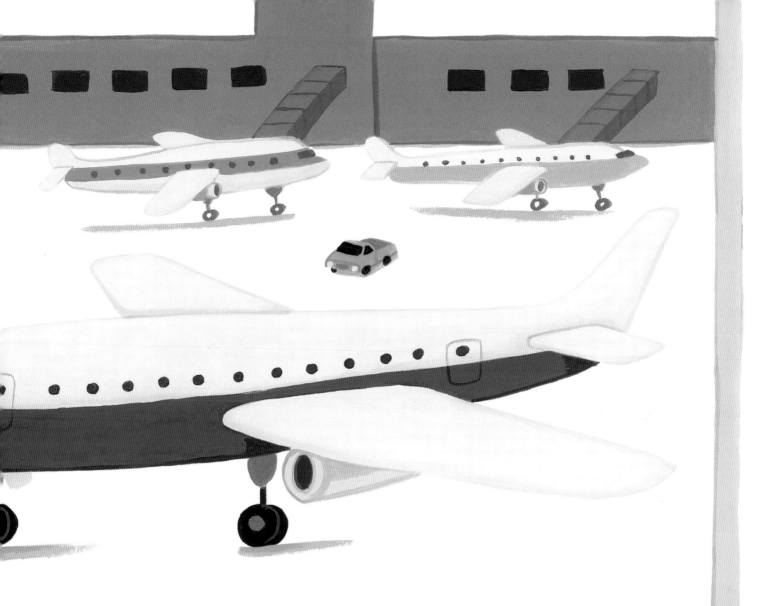

"Through a special tunnel," said Mummy. "You will
see when it's our turn to get on the plane."

The loudspeaker voice announced that Topsy
and Tim's aeroplane was ready. Soon they were
walking along a telescopic tunnel and stepping
into the aeroplane. It looked like a very long bus.

"Welcome aboard," said the
stewardess to Topsy and Tim.

The stewardess helped Topsy and
Tim fasten their safety belts.
She gave them some comics
and some sweets.

"Suck a sweet when the aeroplane starts to fly,"
she said. "It will stop your ears hurting."
Tim took two sweets.
"One for each ear," he said.
The stewardess laughed.
"They go in your mouth,
not your ears!" she said.

The big aeroplane flew up into the sky.
Topsy and Tim watched trees and houses grow as
small as toys.
"My ears have gone funny," said Topsy.
"You didn't suck your sweet, that's why," said Tim.

Topsy and Tim were flying above the clouds.
"Isn't this exciting!" said Mummy.
But the clouds went on for miles and miles.
Topsy and Tim began to fidget.

Lunch came in interesting plastic trays.
Each piece of food had its own shaped space like
the pieces of a jigsaw puzzle. Topsy and Tim tried to
swap pieces. The stewardess had to clear up the mess.
Then she said, "Topsy and Tim, the pilot would like
to talk to you."

The stewardess took Topsy and Tim to the pilot's cabin.
"Hello twins," said the pilot. "I've been hearing about you."
He showed Topsy and Tim all the switches and levers and
dials he used to fly the aeroplane.
"Do you think you could fly my aeroplane?" asked the pilot.
Topsy and Tim were not sure.

They went back to their seats and fastened their safety
belts once more. Then they pretended to be pilots.
"Will you land our aeroplane now, please, pilots?"
asked the stewardess.

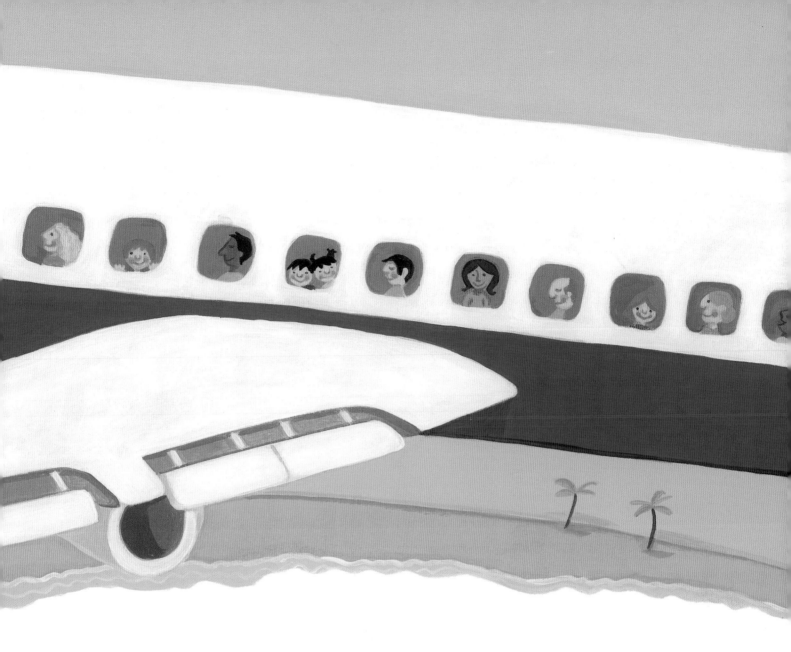

Topsy and Tim could see the flaps moving in the
aeroplane's wings to make it fly lower.
"I'm doing that when I move this lever," said Tim.
But Topsy and Tim both knew the real pilot was doing it.

Topsy and Tim's aeroplane landed with hardly a bump.

"Goodbye everybody," said Topsy and Tim.
They waved goodbye to the stewardess and to the
pilot up in the aeroplane's nose. Then they went to
meet their luggage on another moving platform.

Soon Topsy and Tim were
playing on a sunny holiday beach.
A big aeroplane flew across the sky.
"That's our plane going home," said Tim.
Topsy and Tim waved to their aeroplane –
and they thought it waggled its
wings back at them.

Now turn the page and help
Topsy and Tim solve a puzzle.

Topsy and Tim are looking down from the aeroplane.
They are trying to spot these things:

- two red tractors
- two windmills
- one church
- three horses

Can you spot them, too?

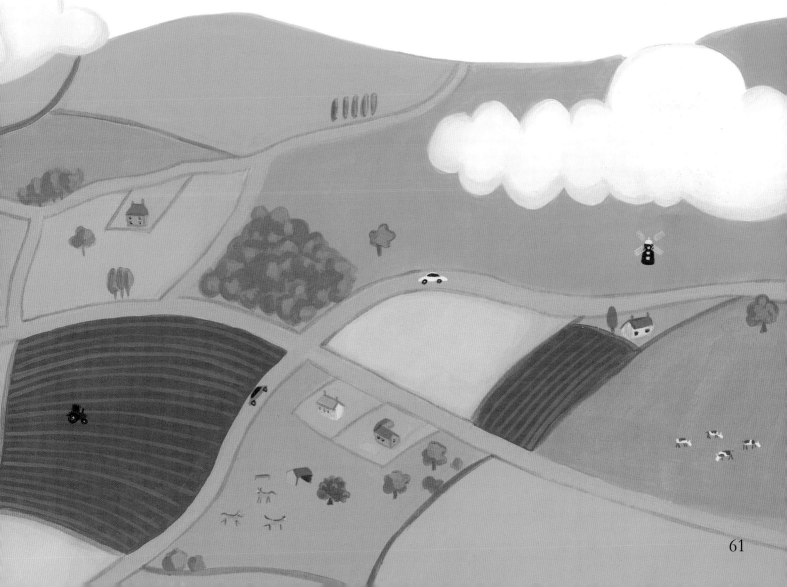

Topsy and Tim Start School

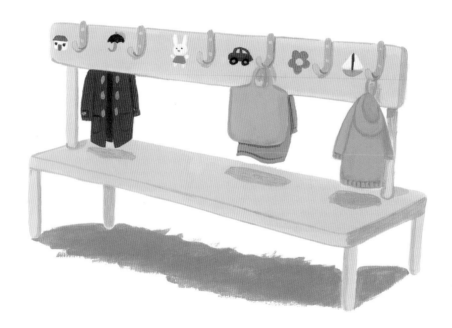

Tiddlywinks
Nursery

Topsy and Tim were off to school after a fantastic
summer holiday. They felt happy and excited.
They walked straight past their old nursery.

Topsy and Tim were going to join the bigger children at the Primary School. They knew the Primary School was a cheerful, friendly place. They had been there already, on a visit. But Topsy and Tim held hands as they went through the big gateway.

65

"Oh, look," said Tim.
"There's Tony Welch."
"Hi, Tony!" called Topsy,
but her voice came out not
quite loud enough.

The Primary School was much noisier than their old nursery. Some of the bigger children did look very big. Topsy and Tim soon met several of their old friends, as well as Tony.

Miss Terry was
Topsy and Tim's
class teacher.

She showed them where to hang their coats and bags.
Each peg had a different picture by it.
"Remember your special picture," said Miss Terry,
"and then you will know your own peg."

"My peg's got a rabbit like Wiggles," said Topsy.
Tim's peg had a picture of a black umbrella.

He wasn't sure he could remember an old umbrella.
"Girls always get the best things," grumbled Tim.

Mummy took Topsy and Tim into their new classroom.

"There's Tony again," said Topsy. They went to see what he was doing.

Tony was busy doing a jigsaw puzzle.
"Would you like to do a jigsaw puzzle,
Topsy and Tim?" said Miss Terry.

Topsy and Tim found plenty of interesting things to do.
There was sand to dig in and water for sailing and sploshing.
The home corner had scales that worked.

When they felt like looking at books
and pictures, they sat on the carpet in
the quiet corner. The bell for playtime
seemed to ring too soon.

Miss Terry led the children into the school playground. It was full of big boys and girls all making a noise.

Topsy and Tim stayed close to
Miss Terry for a while.

Soon Topsy and Tim were playing happily with some new friends. Then a big boy rang a loud bell. Everybody stopped playing and stood in lines to go back into school.

78

Dinner was served by two jolly ladies, Miss Knitting and Mrs Pie. At least, Topsy and Tim thought those were their names. Topsy was astonished to see Tim eat all his greens.

Afternoon school was more like their old nursery. Miss Terry gathered all the children round her. They sang some clever songs, with actions.

When it was time to go home, Topsy and Tim went
to put on their jackets.
"I can remember my peg picture," said Tim proudly.
"It's an umbrella."
But Tim's peg was empty. Tim was upset.

"Never mind, Tim," said Miss Terry. "This often
happens. I expect someone knocked your things
down and put them back on the
wrong peg by mistake."

"Here's your jacket,"
called Andy Anderson.

"Did you enjoy your first
day at big school?" asked
Mummy on the way home.
"Of course we did!" said
Topsy and Tim.

*Now turn the page and help
Topsy and Tim solve a puzzle.*

All the children have their own peg for their coats and bags.
Read the clues. Can you work out which peg belongs to
which child?

Topsy's
peg has a
picture of
something
white and
fluffy.

Tim's peg
has a picture
of something
that is useful in
the rain.

The picture on
Stevie's peg is
of something
fast and red.

The picture on
Vinda's peg is
of something
you can live in.

Tony's peg has a picture of something that floats on water.

Kerry's peg has a picture of something pretty and pink.

Topsy and Tim
Go to the Doctor

It was a cold and misty morning. Mummy cooked a tasty hot breakfast for Topsy and Tim.
"Don't want any breakfast," said Tim.

"Oh, you are a misery,"
said Mummy crossly.
Dad was not cross, but
then he had not cooked
the breakfast.

"This isn't like Tim," he said.
"There must be something wrong.
Open your mouth wide, Tim."
Tim's throat was swollen and red.
"Poor old Tim," said Dad.

Mummy phoned the Health Centre. She made an appointment for Tim to see Dr Sims. They walked to the Health Centre. Tim wore his scarf up over his nose to keep his sore throat warm.

Health Centre

93

The receptionist checked Tim's appointment on her computer.
She told them to go and wait outside Dr Sims' surgery.
"Look," said Topsy. "There's Kerry."
Kerry was one of Topsy and Tim's school friends.

"What's the matter, Kerry?" asked Topsy.
"It hurts when I swallow," Kerry said.
"Tim has a sore throat too," said Topsy.
Tim just looked glum.

Soon it was Tim's turn to go into the surgery.
"Good morning," said Dr Sims.

"Good morning, Dr Sims," said Topsy.
Tim said nothing.
"Tim isn't talking," Topsy explained.
"I think it's because his throat hurts."

"Open your mouth, Tim," said Dr Sims, "and let me see."
Dr Sims took a little flat stick and held it on Tim's tongue.
"Say ah," he said.

Then he looked at Tim's eyes and inside his ears.
"You must have bad ear-ache too, Tim," he said.
Tim nodded.
"You're a brave lad," said Dr Sims.

"Mmm," said Dr Sims. "Up with your jumper, young man."
He put his stethoscope into his ears and listened to
Tim's chest.

"What does that do?" asked Tim.

"I can hear what chests and tummies are saying through it," said Dr Sims. "The sound tells me if people are ill."

Then he let Topsy listen to Tim's heart.

Dr Sims wrote a prescription and gave it to Mummy. "One spoonful four times a day," he said. "This will soon make you feel better, Tim."

Mummy took Topsy and Tim to the Chemist's.
Mrs White, the pharmacist, prepared Tim's
medicine and gave it to Mummy.
"Make sure he takes all the medicine," she said.

Mummy put the medicine safely in her bag.
Just then, Kerry came past.
"I've got some medicine," she said.
"Tim's got some too," said Topsy.

When they got home, Mummy took out the medicine.
It had a special childproof top, but Mummy could
open it. She poured out a spoonful for Tim.
"Did it taste nice?" asked Topsy.
"Mmm," said Tim, licking his lips.

Then Mummy locked the bottle of medicine away
in a cupboard, out of Topsy and Tim's reach.

When Dad came home, Tim was tucking into
blackcurrant jelly. Topsy was not eating hers.
"She's sulking because she isn't ill," said Tim.
"I wonder," said Dad. "Open wide, Topsy,
and let Dr Dad have a look."
Topsy's throat was red and sore.

Dad took Topsy to the Health Centre that evening. Her throat was sore but she was proud to be going to see the doctor.

Dr Sims was not there, so Topsy saw Dr Jaunty instead.
She came home with a bottle of medicine just like Tim's.

*Now turn the page and help
Topsy and Tim solve a puzzle.*

Look at the two pictures.
There are six differences.
Can you spot them all?

Topsy and Tim
Go Camping

Topsy and Tim were going camping with
Mummy and Dad. They were taking two
tents – a big one for Mummy and Dad and
a small one for Topsy and Tim.

It was a long drive, but at last they arrived at the
campsite. It was in a field, beside a little wood.
Topsy and Tim helped to unload the car.

Putting the tents up was a puzzle at first, but Topsy and Tim soon remembered how to do it.
"I like our tent best," said Topsy.

Tim went to fetch water. He was surprised to find a tap in the field. It was a very splashy tap.

There was hot soup for supper and sandwiches
and big red apples.

After supper, Topsy and Tim went with Mummy
and Dad to explore the wood.
"Somebody's been painting arrows on the trees,"
said Tim. "Look!"

"Yes," said Mummy. "If we follow those arrows, they will take us for a good walk and bring us back to camp."

When they got back to their camp they saw that another
family had arrived in the field – two big boys and their
mum and dad. They were unloading their car and putting
up their tent.

The big boys were very noisy.

"Let's go and play inside our tent," said Topsy to Tim.

"It's time you two got into your sleeping bags,"
said Mummy.

Topsy and Tim were almost asleep in their cosy sleeping bags when something hit their tent with a WALLOP! It gave them a fright.

The naughty boys had kicked a football
hard at Topsy and Tim's tent.
"Sorry," called the boys.

Next morning, Topsy and Tim were up bright and early
and so were the big boys.
"We are going to play in the wood," said the big boys.
"We'll come too," said Topsy and Tim.

They had a wonderful time in the wood.
They swung from trees like monkeys.
"I'm the king of the jungle!" shouted Tim.

They chased after rabbits, trying to catch them, but the rabbits ran faster.

"I nearly caught one," puffed Topsy, "but it ran down a rabbit hole."

129

At last they began to feel hungry. None of them
had had breakfast. They wanted to go back to the
camp, but they did not know which way to go.

"We're lost," said one of the big boys.
"No we're not," said Topsy.
"The arrows on the trees will lead us back
to camp. Mummy said so."

131

Mummy and Dad were glad to see them.

"I was just coming to find you," said Dad.

"What have you been up to?"

"We've had adventures," said Tim.

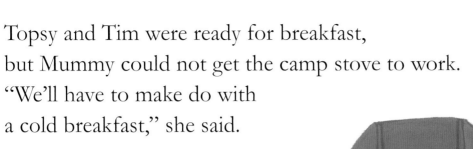

Topsy and Tim were ready for breakfast,
but Mummy could not get the camp stove to work.
"We'll have to make do with
a cold breakfast," she said.

The big boys' dad came to see what was wrong.
"Come and join us," he said. "There's plenty of
room on our barbeque."

Soon there was the lovely smell of sausages and
bacon cooking on the big boys' barbeque –
and there was plenty for everyone.

"I love camping," said Tim.
"I wish we could stay here forever," said Topsy.

*Now turn the page and help
Topsy and Tim solve a puzzle.*

Mummy, Dad, Topsy and Tim are having
supper at the campsite.
Look at the five jigsaw pieces.
Can you work out where each piece will fit?

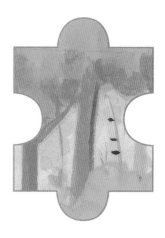
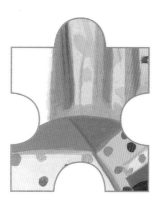
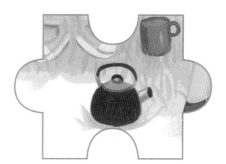

Goodbye, see you soon!

Have you read all the Topsy and Tim stories?

 **Topsy and Tim At the Farm**
Jean and Gareth Adamson
☐ 9781409303367

 **Topsy and Tim Go Camping**
Jean and Gareth Adamson
☐ 9781409303336

 **Topsy and Tim Go on an Aeroplane**
Jean and Gareth Adamson
☐ 9781409300571

 **Topsy and Tim Go on a Train**
Jean and Gareth Adamson
☐ 9781409304241

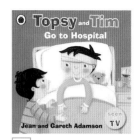 **Topsy and Tim Go to Hospital**
Jean and Gareth Adamson
☐ 9781409304234

 **Topsy and Tim Start School**
Jean and Gareth Adamson
☐ 9781409300830

 **Topsy and Tim Go to the Doctor**
Jean and Gareth Adamson
☐ 9781409303343

 **Topsy and Tim Go to the Dentist**
Jean and Gareth Adamson
☐ 9781409300588

 **Topsy and Tim Have a Birthday Party**
Jean and Gareth Adamson
☐ 9781409300618

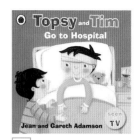 **Topsy and Tim Meet Father Christmas**
Jean and Gareth Adamson
✓ 9781409311591

 **Topsy and Tim Meet the Police**
Jean and Gareth Adamson
☐ 9781409308836

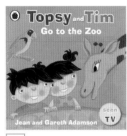 **Topsy and Tim Go to the Zoo**
Jean and Gareth Adamson
☐ 9781409300847

 **Topsy and Tim Meet the Firefighters**
Jean and Gareth Adamson
☐ 9781409307211

 **Topsy and Tim Learn to Swim**
Jean and Gareth Adamson
☐ 9781409300601

 **Topsy and Tim Play Football**
Jean and Gareth Adamson
☐ 9781409303350

 **Topsy and Tim Safety First**
Jean and Gareth Adamson
☐ 9781409308829

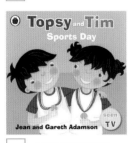 **Topsy and Tim Sports Day**
Jean and Gareth Adamson
☐ 9781409309468

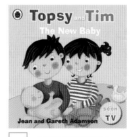 **Topsy and Tim Have Itchy Heads**
Jean and Gareth Adamson
☐ 9781409307204

 **Topsy and Tim The New Baby**
Jean and Gareth Adamson
☐ 9781409300564

 **Topsy and Tim Visit London**
Jean and Gareth Adamson
☐ 9781409309475

 Available on the App Store
 ANDROID APP ON Google play

The Topsy and Tim app is now available
The Topsy and Tim ebook range is available through all digital retailers.